THUNDER
AND LIGHTNING

written by Fiona Campbell *and* Don Harper
illustrated by Studio Boni/Galante
and Ivan Stalio

Ladybird

CONTENTS

IN THE BEGINNING

Storms can be very frightening and destructive, but they may also be the reason that life exists on Earth. There have almost certainly been thunderstorms here since the planet was formed. There is evidence of storms which happened more than 200 million years ago, from changes in the soil caused by ancient lightning strikes.

The intense heat of lightning causes the oxygen and nitrogen gases in the air to combine together to form **nitrate**. This could have been used as food by the first tiny forms of life.

WINDY WEATHER

Wind is moving air. When air is heated, it becomes lighter and then rises. Cooler air from surrounding areas moves in to take the place of the rising air. This air movement forms wind. When wind blows, it brings different types of weather with it.

Heat from the Sun
The Sun's rays heat the Earth's surface. But, dust in the Earth's **atmosphere** from pollution and volcanic eruptions can reduce the amount of heat reaching the Earth. The dust acts like a barrier, reflecting heat back into space.

Warm air rises

Air rising in one place may form winds far away.

Cooler air moves in, forming a wind.

The strength of a wind depends on how fast the heated air rises. When air rises quickly, surrounding air rushes in to take its place. This forms strong, blustery winds. Light, gentle breezes happen when heated air rises slowly.

About 10,000 metres high in the atmosphere, there are areas of strong winds called jet streams. Jet streams help to move hot air from the Equator towards the poles, keeping the Earth at a more even temperature.

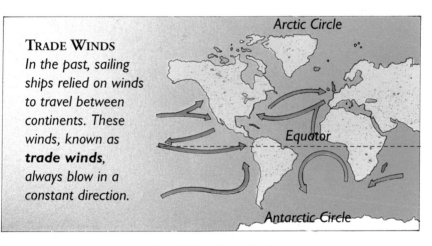

TRADE WINDS
In the past, sailing ships relied on winds to travel between continents. These winds, known as **trade winds,** *always blow in a constant direction.*

Arctic Circle

Equator

Antarctic Circle

Catching the wind
In parts of the sea close to the Equator, there is sometimes hardly any wind. Sailing ships can be dangerously becalmed in these areas of no wind, which are known as the **doldrums**.

CLOUDS AND RAIN

When water in rivers, lakes and seas is heated by the Sun, some of the water **evaporates** to form **water vapour**. As air rises, the water vapour cools and **condenses** onto pieces of dust in the air, forming tiny droplets of water that accumulate into clouds. When these drops of water fall from the cloud, it rains.

Clouds
Clouds are made up of millions of tiny water droplets.

A rain droplet
Water droplets in a cloud are thrown around by air currents. The droplets bump into each other, and grow bigger and bigger.

Rainfall
When water droplets in a cloud become too heavy, they fall as rain.

Clouds vary in size and shape, and they form layers in the sky. Cirrus and cirro-type clouds occur at altitudes above 7,500 metres. Alto-type clouds form lower down at heights of about 3,000 metres. Clouds can help to forecast the weather. For example, the appearance of cumulonimbus clouds indicates the approach of a storm.

Kinds of clouds

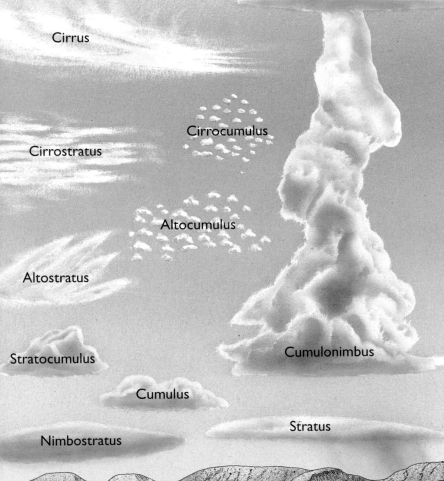

Cirrus

Cirrocumulus

Cirrostratus

Altocumulus

Altostratus

Stratocumulus

Cumulonimbus

Cumulus

Stratus

Nimbostratus

HEATING THE EARTH

The Earth is surrounded by a mixture of gases which form our atmosphere. The atmosphere is made up of several layers. The lowest layer is called the **troposphere** and contains the air that surrounds us. Movement of air within this layer brings different weather conditions. The ozone layer, which helps to protect us against harmful radiation from the Sun, occurs above the troposphere.

The layers of the atmosphere

Where air is thin
The air temperature falls dramatically in the lower layers of the atmosphere. In the **mesosphere**, the air temperature is as low as -173°C.

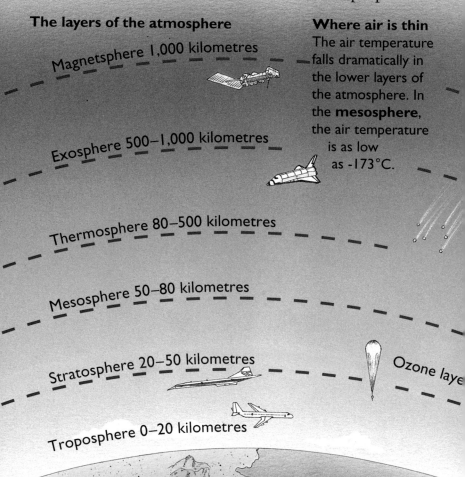

Magnetsphere 1,000 kilometres

Exosphere 500–1,000 kilometres

Thermosphere 80–500 kilometres

Mesosphere 50–80 kilometres

Stratosphere 20–50 kilometres

Ozone layer

Troposphere 0–20 kilometres

The Sun gives out huge amounts of energy, called **solar radiation**, which is made up of different types of rays. About 30 per cent of solar radiation is reflected straight back into space. The remaining 70 per cent warms the air, powers the weather systems on Earth and is used by plants to create energy for photosynthesis.

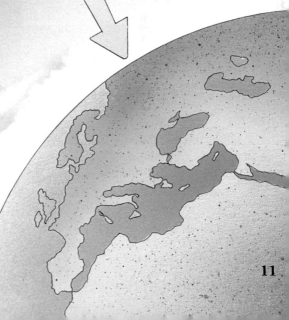

The greenhouse effect
A build up of gases, such as carbon dioxide, from Earth is occurring in the atmosphere. Although the Sun's rays can reach the Earth, the gases are forming a barrier to prevent heat escaping, acting like the glass in a greenhouse. This effect creates **global warming**.

Our Sun
Temperatures on the surface of the Sun may be as high as 6,000°C.

Reflection
Clouds reflect some of the Sun's rays back into space.

Increasing storms
A global temperature rise of one degree Celsius could mean that there will be five times as many thunderstorms than there are now.

SOLAR SYSTEM STORMS

The Earth is not the only planet where there is thunder and lightning. Storms may occur on some of the other planets in the Solar System. Signs of thunderstorms have been seen on photographs relayed back through space to Earth by satellites and spacecraft.

Jupiter

The *Voyager* spaceprobes flew past Jupiter in 1979 and detected huge lightning flashes and storms in the Jovian atmosphere. The *Great Red Spot* may itself be a storm so big that it could swallow three planets the size of the Earth.

Mars

Lightning is generated in dust storms on Mars. It forms in the same way as it does in sandstorms on Earth – by particles of sand rubbing together.

Mercury

Earth

Sun

Venus

In 1978, *Pioneer* spaceprobes found thick clouds of sulphuric acid droplets floating 50 kilometres high in a thick Venusian atmosphere. Beneath the clouds, there is gloomy darkness lit only by flashes of great thunder and lightning storms.

There is no lightning on Mercury or on our Moon, because they have no atmosphere. Nobody knows for sure whether there are thunderstorms on the outer planets – Uranus, Neptune and Pluto.

Neptune
Winds on Neptune blow ten times faster than hurricane force winds on Earth, making Neptune the windiest place in the Solar System.

Pluto

Uranus

Saturn
Saturn is like Jupiter, but smaller and less active. It also has thunderstorms.

Storms on the Sun
Storms do occur on the Sun. They consist of ultra-hot gas that sweeps outwards in a powerful wind that affects the whole family of planets.

SPARKS OF LIGHTNING

Water droplets are changed into small ice particles as they are blown upwards in the sky and become frozen. Within a storm cloud, there is a layer of heavy ice balls through which smaller particles of ice are blown. As the particles hit the ice balls, there is a separation of electrical charge into positive and negative particles. This builds up and causes sheet lightning in the cloud.

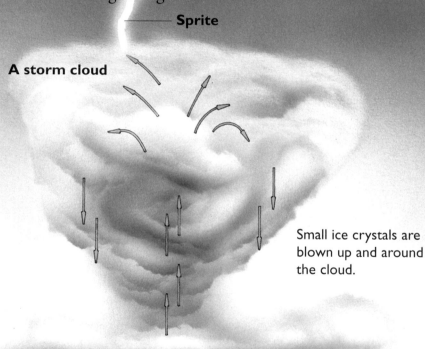

—— **Sprite**

A storm cloud

Small ice crystals are blown up and around the cloud.

Sprites
Brief flashes of light, known as **sprites**, have been seen above storm clouds. We do not know what causes a sprite.

Lightning begins as a small spark in a thundercloud. As it travels towards Earth, the spark connects up with an object here. When this link is made, the effect is similar to turning on a light switch. The lightning strikes the ground and can pass down through it. The light actually moves upwards from the ground, towards the sky.

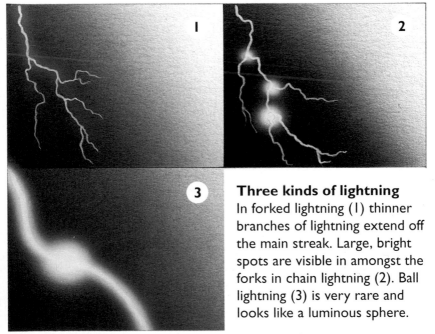

Three kinds of lightning
In forked lightning (1) thinner branches of lightning extend off the main streak. Large, bright spots are visible in amongst the forks in chain lightning (2). Ball lightning (3) is very rare and looks like a luminous sphere.

WHAT IS LIGHTNING?

Thunder and lightning both happen at the same time, but you see lightning before you hear thunder because light travels much faster than sound.

Today, many high buildings are protected from being struck by lightning by metal rods called **conductors**. The lightning is channelled along the rod and through a cable so that it drains away safely into the ground, rather than damaging the building.

A shocking experience
Benjamin Franklin, an American statesman and scientist, was the first person to prove that lightning was a form of electricity, by a dangerous experiment. He flew a kite, made from a silk handkerchief, in a storm and saw how the sparks flew from the string to the metal key attached to it, and then on to his hand. His research led to the development of the first lightning conductor, in 1753.

An electrical spark
Lightning is simply a gigantic electrical spark. Sparks may occur in the clouds, producing sheet lightning, or they may move from a cloud to the ground, causing forked lightning.

FORECASTING A STORM

Helium-filled balloons are used
to lift instruments high into
the atmosphere. These
instruments gather
information, such as
the size of water
droplets in clouds.
They help to detect
atmospheric changes
which indicate an
oncoming storm.

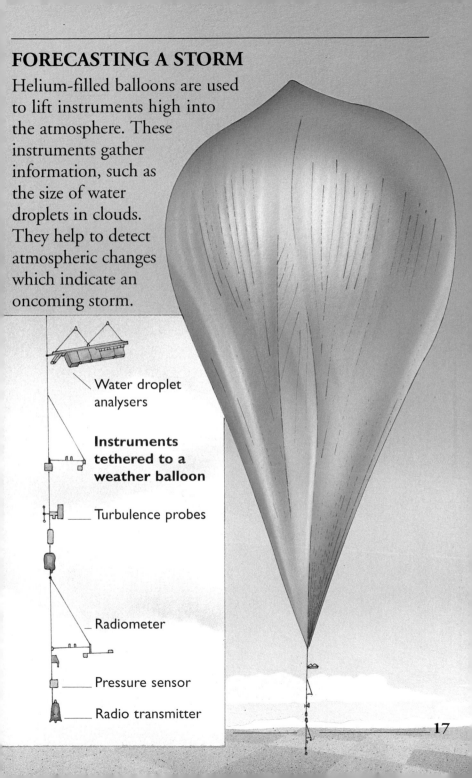

Water droplet
analysers

**Instruments
tethered to a
weather balloon**

Turbulence probes

Radiometer

Pressure sensor

Radio transmitter

STAYING SAFE IN A STORM

One of the safest places to be in a thunderstorm is in a car. Metal has a low resistance to electricity, so the electricity will flow through the metal rather than passing inside the car and hurting the people inside.

When the rains come after the storm, the burnt grassland starts to be transformed. The fire cleared the ground of dead vegetation, and seeds in the soil now sprout into life. *Banksia* seeds actually need to be burnt out of their seed capsules before they will start to grow in the fresh soil.

The ash left by the fire acts as fertilizer for the young plants. Larger trees which may have been burnt by the fire now start to grow new shoots and leaves. The area becomes green and animals return here to feed on the fresh vegetation. Soon however, the ground dries out, as the dry season begins again.

AVOIDING DANGER

If you find yourself out in a thunderstorm and you cannot get inside a vehicle, crouch down with your legs together. This should help to protect you, as lightning usually strikes the tallest object around. People can survive being hit by lightning, provided that it misses both the heart and the central nervous system.

FLYING IN A STORM

Pilots try to avoid thunderstorms but sometimes it is impossible to fly around a storm. On average, every airliner will be struck about once a year. In almost all cases, a plane acts like a metal case and the lightning passes safely through it.

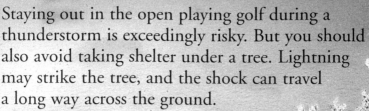

Staying out in the open playing golf during a thunderstorm is exceedingly risky. But you should also avoid taking shelter under a tree. Lightning may strike the tree, and the shock can travel a long way across the ground.

There is also the possibility that the tree will explode. This happens because the liquid sap inside the tree boils as a result of the heat of the lightning.

BENEFITS OF A NATURAL STORM

Lightning strikes will ignite dry vegetation, and cause fires. This is most common in tropical parts of the world, such as the grasslands of Africa. Here, plants and animals have adapted to survive these fires.

As the fire spreads, it catches the dry grass and burns very quickly, moving on, often being driven by strong winds. The direction of the fire may change as a result of the prevailing winds.

It is always a good idea not to be trapped outdoors in a storm. Lightning kills about 400 people every year in America alone. Storms bring other dangers, such as falling trees, floods and high seas.

STAYING SAFE INSIDE

Speaking on the telephone with a storm overhead can be dangerous because lightning may pass down the line to the metal earpiece.

It is wise to disconnect the television aerial because if this is struck by lightning, it may blow up your television set and cause a fire.

Fishing is dangerous

Stop fishing when there is a thunderstorm. Simply holding the fishing rod up can attract a lightning strike, and act as a conductor, passing the electricity through your body.

Some animals can escape more easily from lightning fires than others. Most birds can fly away, but some birds, such as storks, stay around the edges of the flames. Here, they can catch small animals like lizards trying to run to safety.

Slow moving tortoises cannot outrun the fire, so they retreat into their shells when the flames reach them. Tortoises are unlikely to be harmed because they are protected by their shells and the thick scales on their feet mean they can walk safely on the cooling embers.

THE SOUND OF THUNDER

Thunder is caused by lightning and is really hot air exploding. A flash of lightning is extremely hot and as it travels, it makes the air around it expand and contract very quickly, causing the loud rumbling crash or crack of thunder.

Thunderbird

North American Indians believed thunder was caused by huge thunderbirds, which rose up in the sky and caused the noise by flapping their wings.

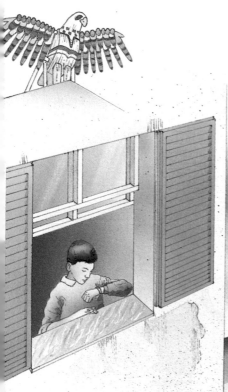

Thor

In Scandinavia, the Norse god Thor was said to cause thunder with his hammer, battling with giants in the skies.

Measuring a storm

You can measure how far away a storm is by counting the seconds between the flash of lightning and the sound of thunder. Dividing the number of seconds by three will then tell you how near or how far away the storm is, in kilometres.

HURRICANES, TYPHOONS AND CYCLONES

In tropical areas where the air is hot and moist, thunderstorms over the warm sea sometimes develop into violent, whirling storms called hurricanes. In the North Pacific Ocean and the China Sea they are called **typhoons**, and elsewhere they are known as **cyclones**. When a hurricane is forecast, people living in coastal areas often evacuate their houses and go inland. Hurricanes usually die out soon after hitting land.

In the eye of a storm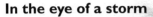
In the centre of the storm is a calm, quiet area called the eye.

HURRICANE DAMAGE
Hurricanes cause a great deal of damage. They occur in warm, tropical areas (1). Heavy rain and huge waves can flood the land near coasts (2). Fierce winds batter and destroy buildings and trees (3).

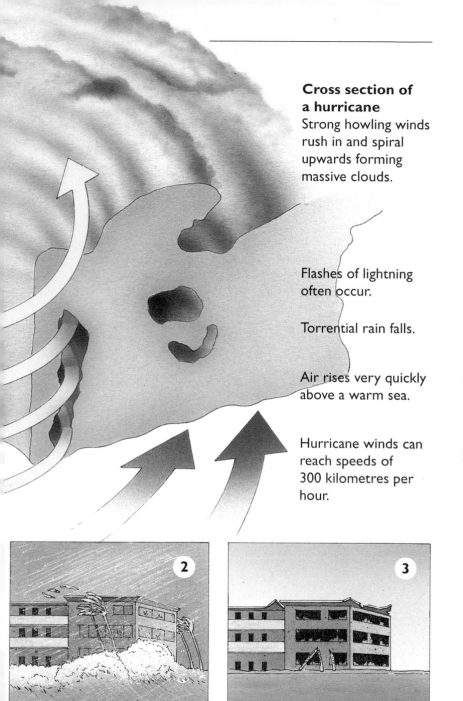

Cross section of a hurricane
Strong howling winds rush in and spiral upwards forming massive clouds.

Flashes of lightning often occur.

Torrential rain falls.

Air rises very quickly above a warm sea.

Hurricane winds can reach speeds of 300 kilometres per hour.

2

3

FROST AND SNOW

On clear nights, as the air cools, droplets of water called **dew** form on leaves and grass. But on very cold, cloudless nights the ground temperature falls below freezing. Then the water vapour in the air freezes as it condenses onto cold surfaces, covering everything with a layer of thick, sparkling frost.

Frost
Patterns of frost appear on cold surfaces such as windows, as the droplets of water on the glass turn into ice.

Snowflakes are formed from ice crystals that join together in very cold clouds. If the air is warm, these snowflakes will melt into rain, but if the air is cold, they will stay as snow. Scientists believe that different weather conditions produce different shaped ice crystals.

Snowflakes

All snowflakes are different. Most are like six-pronged stars, but some are pointed, like needles, or flat like plates.

Needles

Stars

Plates

TORNADOES

Very dangerous whirlwinds, known as tornadoes or twisters, can cause terrible damage when they strike. Powerful tornadoes have been known to lift cars, destroy buildings and overturn trains. Tornadoes can vary in size from just a few metres to 500 metres across.

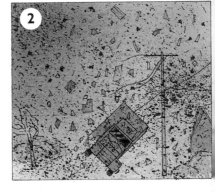

Tornado damage

People who live in areas prone to tornadoes are warned of oncoming damage (1) and take cover in a tornado cellar.

The rapid fall of pressure as a tornado sucks air in causes buildings to explode (2), leaving total devastation (3).

Tornadoes often occur in the mid-western states of America on hot **humid** days where warm, moist air is blowing from different directions. A tornado begins as a funnel-shaped cloud, which stretches down from the base of a huge thundercloud and rotates violently. It soon reaches the ground where there is a deafening roar of upsurging winds.

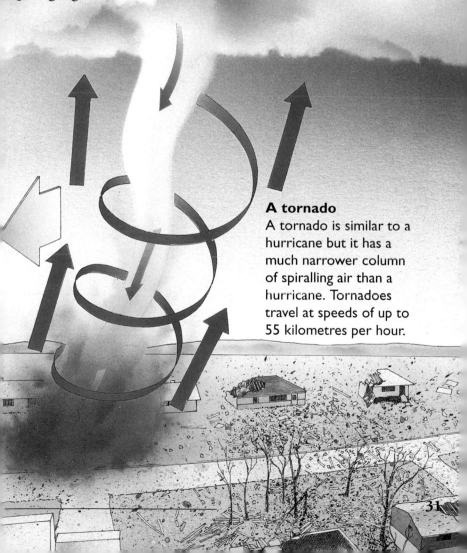

A tornado
A tornado is similar to a hurricane but it has a much narrower column of spiralling air than a hurricane. Tornadoes travel at speeds of up to 55 kilometres per hour.

FLOODS

Floods occur when very heavy rain falls, resulting in so much water that it cannot seep into the soil or flow away into rivers and lakes, or run away into drains. Floods can also happen when rivers swell and burst their banks, or coastal areas are hit by massive storm waves, or large amounts of snow melt quickly.

Many people still choose to live in areas at risk from floods. Often the soil near riverbanks is very rich and good for growing crops. Barriers can sometimes help to protect people against floods.

CHANGING CLIMATES

Long ago, the Earth's **climates** were different from those of today. There have been times, called ice ages, when it was much colder than it is now and huge ice sheets covered many countries. There have also been times when it was hotter and more humid than today, and the land was covered in forests.

Ice Ages

During the ice ages, much of the Earth was covered in ice and animals such as the woolly mammoth roamed the frozen land. Today, ice sheets are only found at the poles.

Woolly mammoth

The ozone layer

There is a layer of ozone found about 50 kilometres high in the atmosphere. Ozone is simply a form of oxygen and it protects us from some of the Sun's harmful rays. But pollution is destroying the ozone layer and its protective effects. The hole in the ozone layer is most prominent around the South Pole.

WEATHER WATCHING

In the past, before technology was used to monitor the weather accurately, people looked at the skies, watched how animals and plants behaved, and relied on signs and superstitions to forecast the weather. For example, some people still believe that when cows lie down or a cat sneezes, it is going to rain.

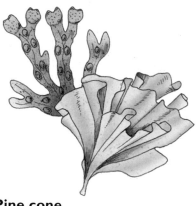

Seaweed
People used to keep seaweed to help forecast the weather. Seaweed feels damp and limp in wet weather, and crispy and dry in the Sun.

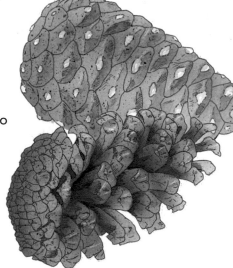

Pine cone
Pine cones predict the weather by closing up in the cold, and opening up when it is warmer to let the seeds fall out.

Spider's web
Spiders are said to start spinning their webs before windy weather.

Nowadays, scientists who study the weather, called meteorologists, use many different methods to make their forecasts. Satellites monitor our weather and send information to computers at special processing stations. On the ground, weather stations all over the world record wind speeds and directions, temperature, clouds and **air pressure**.

Satellites
Weather satellites record the Earth's atmosphere. They transmit photographs daily and are very useful in detecting hurricanes.

Radar
Radar stations on the ground pick up and transmit information round the world.

Balloons
Instruments aboard gas-filled balloons record weather conditions.

Stevenson's screen
This screen provides weather information at ground level.

USING COMPUTERS
People at weather stations record the temperature, humidity and pressure every few hours. Powerful computers analyse these recordings to forecast the weather.

AMAZING THUNDER & LIGHTNING FACTS

- **Fire in the sky** Fireballs are a rare form of lightning occasionally seen during thunderstorms on high trees or masts of ships. They are reddish in colour, range in size from an orange to a football and last less than a minute.

- **Power source** The power of a lightning flash is equivalent to 100 million volts, which is enough to light a small town for several weeks.

- **Greatest survivor** Park ranger Roy Sullivan, of Virginia, America, was first hit by lightning in 1942. He was then struck another six times up until 1977. He only had minor injuries – burnt eyebrows, hair and legs, and the loss of a toenail.

- **Heat generation** The heat generated by lightning may be five times hotter than the surface of the Sun.

- **Thunderstorms on Earth** Today on Earth, about 1,800 thunderstorms strike constantly at different points around the globe, every single second of every day. There are also about 6,000 lightning flashes every minute. There are more than 40 million lightning strikes in America alone every year.

- **Explosions in the air** Early airships built in the 1930s often exploded if hit by lightning. Just a tiny spark would ignite the highly inflammable hydrogen gas in the balloon.

- **Speed of lightning** Lightning travels at a speed close to 1,600 kilometres per second to Earth, and the flashes can be as long as 140 kilometres.

- **Stormy planet** The winds on the planet Neptune are so fast, they almost break the sound barrier.

GLOSSARY

Air pressure The weight of the atmosphere pushing down on the surface of the Earth.

Atmosphere The mixture of gases, made up of layers, which surround the Earth.

Climate The average weather conditions of a particular place.

Condense When a gas cools down to a certain temperature and becomes a liquid.

Conductor Materials like metal or water which allow electricity to flow through them.

Cyclone A tropical storm with very strong winds and heavy rain.

Dew Moisture which forms on the ground overnight, especially on grass, when the weather is clear and not windy.

Doldrums Region of sea close to the Equator with little or no wind.

Evaporation A process where water is heated and is transformed from a liquid into water vapour.

Global warming An increase in the temperature of the Earth's atmosphere.

Humid When the air is warm and full of moisture.

Mesosphere The part of the upper atmosphere, at heights of 50 to 80 kilometres, where meteors from outer space usually burn up before they reach the Earth.

Nitrate A combination of nitrogen and oxygen, which can be used as a fertilizer.

Solar radiation The heat and light that come from the Sun.

Sprite A brief spurt of light above a thundercloud, which was first seen by aircraft pilots.

Trade winds The constant winds blowing north and south towards the Equator.

Troposphere The layer of the atmosphere that surrounds us, up to a height of twenty kilometres. Storms and other weather changes take place in this layer.

Typhoon The name given to storms which occur off the coast of Asia, in the North Pacific Ocean and China Sea.

Water vapour An invisible gas which is formed when water is heated.

INDEX *(Entries in **bold** refer to an illustration)*